little senses

Stories for wonderfully sensitive kids, especially those on the autism spectrum and/or with sensory processing issues

It Was Supposed to Be Sunny

by Samantha Cotterill

 Dial Books for Young Readers

Rumble
Rumble...

Boom!

It can't rain! I promised Suzie and Max a sparkly sunshine celebration . . .

A sparkly
SUNSHINE
celebration!

I know the rain is upsetting, Laila.
But I promise it will still be fun!

There are things we can control . . .

and others we cannot.

**Changing plans can be hard,
but sometimes surprises are fun.**

Remember the time we got lost in the car?

We still made it home, and discovered our favorite new shop!

You have been through change before

and you can do it again.

Go unicorn go!

Rumble

Rumble...

CRASH!

My unicorn cake!

It's going to be okay, we can fix this.
For now, let's make unicorn crowns!

Yeeesss!

Yeesss . . .

Mommy?

I don't want to make crowns.
We were supposed to have cake first.
My tummy hurts and I want
everyone to go home.

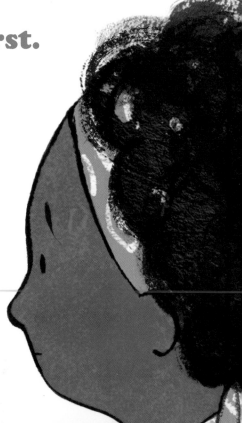

Laila, I know this wasn't part of the plan, but your party can still be great.

Why don't you have a little quiet time with Charlie while I adjust the schedule and get the others started on the crowns.

I've been through this before . . .

and I can do it again.

I've been through this before . . .

and I
CAN
do it again.

I have an idea . . .

What a perfect solution!

Laila's birthday schedule!

- wake up.
- get ready
- set up party ~~outside~~ inside
- friends arrive!
- unicorn obstacle run
- unicorn crown
- ~~unicorn cones~~ cake + wish jar
- sunshine craft!

These unicorn cones
are awesome!

Happy birthday, Laila!

Happy birthday!

Sparkly...

Sunshine....

Celebration!

For Mummsy

Dial Books for Young Readers
An imprint of Penguin Random House LLC, New York

First published in the United States of America by Dial Books for Young Readers,
an imprint of Penguin Random House LLC, 2021

Visit us online at penguinrandomhouse.com.

Library of Congress Cataloging-in-Publication Data is available.

Manufactured in China
ISBN 9780525553472

10 9 8 7 6 5 4 3 2 1

Design by Mina Chung • Text set in Futura and Cooper Md